FATHER BROWN MYSTERIES

MYSTERIES

Volume 1

Cover image © Can Stock
Photo / ahasoft
ISBN: 9798370884887

GRACE'S
GIANT PRINT BOOKS

TABLE OF CONTENTS

The Blue Cross

Between the silver ribbon of
morning and the green glittering ribbon of sea, the boat
touched Harwich and let loose
a swarm of folk like flies,
among whom the man we
must follow was by no means
conspicuous—nor wished to
be. There was nothing notable
about him, except a slight

contrast between the holiday gaiety of his clothes and the official gravity of his face. His clothes included a slight, pale grey jacket, a white waistcoat, and a silver straw hat with a grey-blue ribbon. His lean face was dark by contrast, and ended in a curt black beard that looked Spanish and suggested an Elizabethan ruff. He was smoking a cigarette with the seriousness of an idler. There was nothing about him to indicate the fact that the grey jacket covered a loaded revolver, that the white waist-coat covered a police card, or that the straw hat covered one of the most powerful intellects in Europe. For this was Valentin himself, the head of the Paris police and the most famous investigator of the world; and he was coming from Brussels to London to make the greatest arrest of the century.

Flambeau was in England. The police of three countries

had tracked the great criminal at last from Ghent to Brussels, from Brussels to the Hook of Holland; and it was conjectured that he would take some advantage of the unfamiliarity and confusion of the Eucharistic Congress, then taking place in London. Probably he would travel as some minor clerk or secretary connected with it; but, of course, Valentin could not be certain; nobody could be certain about Flambeau.

It is many years now since this colossus of crime suddenly ceased keeping the world in a turmoil; and when he ceased, as they said after the death of Roland, there was a great quiet upon the earth. But in his best days (I mean, of course, his worst) Flambeau was a figure as statuesque and international as the Kaiser. Almost every morning the daily paper announced that he had escaped the consequences of one extraordinary crime by committing another. He was a Gascon of gigantic stature and bodily daring; and the wildest tales were told of his outbursts of athletic humour; how he turned the juge d'instruction upside down and stood him on his head, "to clear his mind"; how he ran down the Rue de Rivoli with a policeman under each arm. It is due to him to say that his fantastic physical strength was generally employed in such bloodless though undignified scenes; his real crimes were chiefly those of ingenious and wholesale robbery. But each of his thefts was almost a new sin, and would make a story by itself. It was he who ran the great Tyrolean Dairy Company in London, with no dairies, no cows, no carts, no milk, but with some thousand subscribers. These he served by the simple operation of moving the little milk cans outside people's doors to the doors of his own customers. It was he who had kept up an unaccountable and close correspondence with a young lady whose whole letter-bag was intercepted, by the extraordinary trick of photographing his messages infinitesimally small upon the slides of a microscope. A sweeping simplicity, however, marked many of his experiments. It is said that he once repainted all the numbers in a street in the dead of night merely to divert one traveller into a trap. It is quite certain that he invented a portable pillar-box, which he put up at corners in quiet suburbs on the chance of strangers dropping postal orders into it. Lastly, he was known to be a startling acrobat; despite his huge figure, he could leap like a grasshopper and melt into the tree-tops like a monkey. Hence the great Valentin, when he set out to find Flambeau, was perfectly aware that his adventures would not end when he had found him.

But how was he to find him? On this the great Valentin's ideas were still in process of settlement.

There was one thing which Flambeau, with all his dexterity of disguise, could not cover, and that was his singular height. If Valentin's quick eye had caught a tall apple-woman, a tall grenadier, or even a tolerably tall duchess, he might have arrested them on the spot. But all along his train there was nobody that

could be a disguised Flambeau, any more than a cat
could be a disguised giraffe.
About the people on the boat
he had already satisfied himself; and the people picked up
at Harwich or on the journey
limited themselves with certainty to six. There was a short
railway official travelling up to
the terminus, three fairly short
market gardeners picked up
two stations afterwards, one
very short widow lady going
up from a small Essex town,

and a very short Roman Catholic priest going up from a small Essex village. When it came to the last case, Valentin gave it up and almost laughed. The little priest was so much the essence of those Eastern flats; he had a face as round and dull as a Norfolk dumpling; he had eyes as empty as the North Sea; he had several brown paper parcels, which he was quite incapable of collecting. The Eucharistic Congress had doubtless sucked out of their local stagnation many such creatures, blind and helpless, like moles disinterred. Valentin was a sceptic in the severe style of France, and could have no love for priests. But he could have pity for them, and this one might have provoked pity in anybody. He had a large, shabby umbrella, which constantly fell on the floor. He did not seem to know which was the right end of his return ticket. He explained with a moon-calf simplicity to every-body in the carriage that he had to be careful, because he had something made of real silver "with blue stones" in one of his brown-paper parcels. His quaint blending of Essex flat-ness with saintly simplicity continuously amused the Frenchman till the priest ar-rived (somehow) at Tottenham with all his parcels, and came back for his umbrella. When he did the last, Valentin even had the good nature to warn him

14

not to take care of the silver by telling everybody about it. But to whomever he talked, Valentin kept his eye open for someone else; he looked out steadily for anyone, rich or poor, male or female, who was well up to six feet; for Flambeau was four inches above it.

He alighted at Liverpool Street, however, quite conscientiously secure that he had not missed the criminal so far. He then went to Scotland Yard to regularise his position and arrange for help in case of need; he then lit another cigarette and went for a long stroll in the streets of London. As he was walking in the streets and squares beyond Victoria, he paused suddenly and stood. It was a quaint, quiet square, very typical of London, full of an accidental stillness. The tall, flat houses round looked at once prosperous and uninhabited; the square of shrubbery in the centre looked as deserted as a green Pacific islet. One of the four sides was much higher than the rest, like a dais; and the line of this side was broken by one of London's admirable accidents—a restaurant that looked as if it had strayed from Soho. It was an unreasonably attractive object, with dwarf plants in pots and long, striped blinds of lemon yellow and white. It stood specially high above the street, and in the usual patchwork way of London, a flight of steps from the street ran up to meet the front door almost as a fire-escape might run up to a first-floor window. Valentin stood and smoked in front of the yellow-white blinds and considered them long.

The most incredible thing about miracles is that they happen. A few clouds in heaven do come together into the staring shape of one human eye. A tree does stand up in the landscape of a doubtful journey in the exact and elaborate shape of a note of interrogation. I have seen both these things myself within the last few days. Nelson does die in the instant of victory; and a man named Williams does quite accidentally murder a man named Williamson; it sounds like a sort of infanticide. In short, there is in life an element of elfin coincidence which people reckoning on the prosaic may perpetually miss. As it has been well expressed in the paradox of Poe, wisdom should reckon on the unforeseen.

Aristide Valentin was unfathomably French; and the French intelligence is intelligence specially and solely. He was not "a thinking machine"; for that is a brainless phrase of modern fatalism and materialism. A machine only is a machine because it cannot think. But he was a thinking man, and a plain man at the same time. All his wonderful successes, that looked like conjuring, had been gained by plodding logic, by clear and commonplace French thought. The French electrify the world not by starting any paradox, they electrify it by carrying out a truism. They carry a truism so far—as in the French Revolution. But exactly because Valentin understood reason, he understood the limits of reason. Only a man who knows nothing of motors talks of motoring without petrol; only a man who knows

nothing of reason talks of rea-
soning without strong,
undisputed first principles. Here
he had no strong first principles. Flambeau had been
missed at Harwich; and if he
was in London at all, he might
be anything from a tall tramp
on Wimbledon Common to a
tall toast-master at the Hotel
Metropole. In such a naked
state of nescience, Valentin
had a view and a method of
his own.

In such cases he reckoned

on the unforeseen. In such cases, when he could not follow the train of the reasonable, he coldly and carefully followed the train of the unreasonable. Instead of going to the right places—banks, police stations, rendez-vous—he systematically went to the wrong places; knocked at every empty house, turned down every cul de sac, went up every lane blocked with rubbish, went round every crescent that led him uselessly out of the way. He defended this crazy course quite logically. He said that if one had a clue this was the worst way; but if one had no clue at all it was the best, because there was just the chance that any oddity that caught the eye of the pursuer might be the same that had caught the eye of the pursued. Somewhere a man must begin, and it had better be just where another man might stop. Something about that flight of steps up to the shop, something about the quietude and quaintness of the restaurant, roused all the detective's rare romantic fancy and made him resolve to strike at random. He went up the steps, and sitting down at a table by the window, asked for a cup of black coffee.

It was half-way through the morning, and he had not breakfasted; the slight litter of other breakfasts stood about on the table to remind him of his hunger; and adding a poached egg to his order, he proceeded musingly to shake some white sugar into his coffee, thinking all the time about Flambeau. He remembered how Flambeau had escaped, once by a pair of nail scissors, and once by a house on fire; once by having to pay for an unstamped letter, and once by getting people to look through a telescope at a comet that might destroy the world. He thought his detective brain as good as the criminal's, which was true. But he fully realised the disadvantage. "The criminal is the creative artist; the detective only the critic," he said with a sour smile, and lifted his coffee cup to his lips slowly, and put it down very quickly. He had put salt in it.

He looked at the vessel from which the silvery powder had come; it was certainly a sugar-basin; as unmistakably meant for sugar as a champagne-bottle for champagne. He wondered why they should keep salt in it. He looked to see if there were any more ortho-dox vessels. Yes; there were two salt-cellars quite full. Per-haps there was some speciality in the condiment in the salt-cellars. He tasted it; it was sugar. Then he looked round at the restaurant with a refreshed air of interest, to see if there were any other traces of that singular artistic taste which puts the sugar in the salt-cellars and the salt in the sugar-basin. Except for an odd splash of some dark fluid on one of the white-papered walls, the whole place appeared neat, cheerful and ordinary. He rang the bell for the waiter.

When that official hurried up, fuzzy-haired and somewhat blear-eyed at that early hour, the detective (who was not without an appreciation of the simpler forms of humour) asked him to taste the sugar and see if it was up to the high reputation of the hotel. The result was that the waiter yawned suddenly and woke up.

"Do you play this delicate joke on your customers every morning?" inquired Valentin. "Does changing the salt and sugar never pall on you as a jest?"

The waiter, when this irony grew clearer, stammeringly assured him that the establishment had certainly no such intention; it must be a most curious mistake. He picked up the sugar-basin and looked at it; he picked up the salt-cellar and looked at that, his face growing more and more bewildered. At last he abruptly excused himself, and hurrying away, returned in a few seconds with the proprietor. The proprietor also examined the sugar-basin and then the salt-cellar; the proprietor also looked bewildered.

Suddenly the waiter seemed

to grow inarticulate with a rush of words.

"I zink," he stuttered eagerly, "I zink it is those two clergy-men."

"What two clergymen?"

"The two clergymen," said the waiter, "that threw soup at the wall."

"Threw soup at the wall?" repeated Valentin, feeling sure this must be some singular Italian metaphor.

"Yes, yes," said the attendant excitedly, and

pointed at the dark splash on the white paper; "threw it over there on the wall."

Valentin looked his query at the proprietor, who came to his rescue with fuller reports.

"Yes, sir," he said, "it's quite true, though I don't suppose it has anything to do with the sugar and salt. Two clergymen came in and drank soup here very early, as soon as the shutters were taken down. They were both very quiet, respectable people; one of them paid the bill and went out; the other, who seemed a slower coach altogether, was some minutes longer getting his things together. But he went at last. Only, the instant before he stepped into the street he de-liberately picked up his cup, which he had only half emp-tied, and threw the soup slap on the wall. I was in the back room myself, and so was the waiter; so I could only rush out in time to find the wall splashed and the shop empty.

It don't do any particular damage, but it was confounded cheek; and I tried to catch the men in the street. They were too far off though; I only noticed they went round the next corner into Carstairs Street."

The detective was on his feet, hat settled and stick in hand. He had already decided that in the universal darkness of his mind he could only follow the first odd finger that pointed; and this finger was odd enough. Paying his bill and clashing the glass doors behind him, he was soon swinging round into the other street.

It was fortunate that even in such fevered moments his eye was cool and quick. Something in a shop-front went by him like a mere flash; yet he went back to look at it. The shop was a popular greengrocer and fruiterer's, an array of goods set out in the open air and plainly ticketed with their names and prices. In the two most prominent compartments were two heaps, of oranges and of nuts respectively. On the heap of nuts lay a scrap of cardboard, on which was written in bold, blue chalk, "Best tangerine oranges, two a penny." On the oranges was the equally clear and exact description, "Finest Brazil nuts, 4d. a lb." M. Valentin looked at these two placards and fancied he had met this highly subtle form of humour before, and that somewhat recently.

He drew the attention of the red-faced fruiterer, who was looking rather sullenly up and down the street, to this inaccuracy in his advertisements. The fruiterer said nothing, but sharply put each card into its proper place. The detective, leaning elegantly on his walking-cane, continued to scrutinise the shop. At last he said, "Pray excuse my apparent irrelevance, my good sir, but I should like to ask you a question in experimental psychology and the association of ideas."

The red-faced shopman regarded him with an eye of menace; but he continued gaily, swinging his cane, "Why," he pursued, "why are two tickets wrongly placed in a greengrocer's shop like a shovel hat that has come to London for a holiday? Or, in case I do not make myself clear, what is the mystical association which connects the idea of nuts marked as oranges with the idea of two clergymen, one tall and the other short?"

The eyes of the tradesman stood out of his head like a snail's; he really seemed for an instant likely to fling himself upon the stranger. At last he stammered angrily: "I don't know what you 'ave to do with it, but if you're one of their friends, you can tell 'em from me that I'll knock their silly 'eads off, parsons or no parsons, if they upset my apples again."

"Indeed?" asked the detective, with great sympathy. "Did they upset your apples?"

"One of 'em did," said the heated shopman; "rolled 'em all over the street. I'd 'ave caught the fool but for havin' to pick 'em up."

"Which way did these parsons go?" asked Valentin.

"Up that second road on the left-hand side, and then across the square," said the other promptly.

"Thanks," replied Valentin, and vanished like a fairy. On the other side of the second square he found a policeman, and said: "This is urgent, constable; have you seen two clergymen in shovel hats?"

The policeman began to chuckle heavily. "I 'ave, sir; and if you arst me, one of 'em was drunk. He stood in the middle of the road that bewildered that—"

"Which way did they go?" snapped Valentin.

"They took one of them yellow buses over there," answered the man; "them that go to Hampstead."

Valentin produced his official card and said very rapidly: "Call up two of your men to come with me in pursuit," and crossed the road with such contagious energy that the ponderous policeman was moved to almost agile obedience. In a minute and a half the French detective was joined on the opposite pavement by an inspector and a man in plain clothes.

"Well, sir," began the former, with smiling importance, "and what may—?"

Valentin pointed suddenly with his cane. "I'll tell you on the top of that omnibus," he said, and was darting and dodging across the tangle of the traffic. When all three sank panting on the top seats of the yellow vehicle, the inspector said: "We could go four times as quick in a taxi."

"Quite true," replied their leader placidly, "if we only had an idea of where we were going."

"Well, where are you going?" asked the other, staring.

Valentin smoked frowningly for a few seconds; then, removing his cigarette, he said: "If you know what a man's doing, get in front of him; but if you want to guess what he's doing, keep behind him. Stray when he strays; stop when he stops; travel as slowly as he.

Then you may see what he saw and may act as he acted. All we can do is to keep our eyes skinned for a queer thing."

"What sort of queer thing do you mean?" asked the inspector.

"Any sort of queer thing," answered Valentin, and relapsed into obstinate silence.

The yellow omnibus crawled up the northern roads for what seemed like hours on end; the great detective would not explain further, and perhaps his assistants felt a silent and growing doubt of his errand. Perhaps, also, they felt a silent and growing desire for lunch, for the hours crept long past the normal luncheon hour, and the long roads of the North London suburbs seemed to shoot out into length after length like an infernal tele-scope. It was one of those journeys on which a man perpetually feels that now at last he must have come to the end of the universe, and then finds he has only come to the beginning of Tufnell Park. London died away in draggled taverns and dreary scrubs, and then was unaccountably born again in blazing high streets and blatant hotels. It was like passing through thirteen separate vulgar cities all just touching each other. But though the winter twilight was already threatening the road ahead of them, the Parisian detective still sat silent and watchful, eyeing the frontage of the streets that slid by on either side. By the time they had left Camden Town behind, the policemen were nearly asleep; at least, they gave something like a jump as Valentin leapt erect, struck a hand on each man's shoulder, and shouted to the driver to stop.

They tumbled down the steps into the road without realising why they had been dislodged; when they looked round for enlightenment they found Valentin triumphantly pointing his finger towards a window on the left side of the road. It was a large window, forming part of the long façade of a gilt and palatial public-house; it was the part reserved for respectable dining, and labelled "Restaurant." This window, like all the rest along the frontage of the hotel, was of frosted and figured glass; but in the middle of it was a big, black smash, like a star in the ice.

"Our cue at last," cried Valentin, waving his stick; "the place with the broken window."

"What window? What cue?" asked his principal assistant. "Why, what proof is there that this has anything to do with them?"

Valentin almost broke his bamboo stick with rage.

"Proof!" he cried. "Good God! the man is looking for proof! Why, of course, the chances are twenty to one that it has nothing to do with them. But what else can we do? Don't you see we must either follow one wild possibility or else go home to bed?" He banged his way into the restaurant, followed by his companions, and they were soon seated at a late luncheon at a little table, and looked at the star of smashed glass from the inside. Not that it was very informative to them even then.

"Got your window broken, I

see," said Valentin to the waiter as he paid the bill.

"Yes, sir," answered the attendant, bending busily over the change, to which Valentin silently added an enormous tip. The waiter straightened himself with mild but unmistakable animation.

"Ah, yes, sir," he said. "Very odd thing, that, sir."

"Indeed?" Tell us about it," said the detective with careless curiosity.

"Well, two gents in black

came in," said the waiter; "two of those foreign parsons that are running about. They had a cheap and quiet little lunch, and one of them paid for it and went out. The other was just going out to join him when I looked at my change again and found he'd paid me more than three times too much. 'Here,' I says to the chap who was nearly out of the door, 'you've paid too much.' 'Oh,' he says, very cool, 'have we?' 'Yes,' I says, and picks up the bill to show him. Well, that was a knock-out."

"What do you mean?" asked his interlocutor.

"Well, I'd have sworn on seven Bibles that I'd put 4s. on that bill. But now I saw I'd put 14s., as plain as paint."

"Well?" cried Valentin, moving slowly, but with burning eyes, "and then?"

"The parson at the door he says all serene, 'Sorry to confuse your accounts, but it'll pay for the window.' 'What window?' I says. 'The one I'm going to break,' he says, and smashed that blessed pane with his umbrella."

All three inquirers made an exclamation; and the inspector said under his breath, "Are we after escaped lunatics?" The waiter went on with some relish for the ridiculous story:

"I was so knocked silly for a second, I couldn't do any-thing. The man marched out of the place and joined his friend just round the corner.

Then they went so quick up Bullock Street that I couldn't catch them, though I ran round the bars to do it."

"Bullock Street," said the detective, and shot up that thoroughfare as quickly as the strange couple he pursued.

Their journey now took them through bare brick ways like tunnels; streets with few lights and even with few windows; streets that seemed built out of the blank backs of everything and everywhere. Dusk was deepening, and it was not easy even for the London policemen to guess in what exact direction they were treading. The inspector, however, was pretty certain that they would eventually strike some part of Hampstead Heath. Abruptly one bulging gas-lit window broke the blue twilight like a bull's-eye lantern; and Valentin stopped an instant before a little garish sweetstuff shop. After an instant's hesitation he went in;

he stood amid the gaudy colours of the confectionery with entire gravity and bought thirteen chocolate cigars with a certain care. He was clearly preparing an opening; but he did not need one.

An angular, elderly young woman in the shop had regarded his elegant appearance with a merely automatic inquiry; but when she saw the door behind him blocked with the blue uniform of the inspector, her eyes seemed to wake up.

"Oh," she said, "if you've come about that parcel, I've sent it off already."

"Parcel?" repeated Valentin; and it was his turn to look inquiring.

"I mean the parcel the gentleman left—the clergyman gentleman."

"For goodness' sake," said Valentin, leaning forward with his first real confession of eagerness, "for Heaven's sake tell us what happened exactly."

"Well," said the woman a little doubtfully, "the clergymen came in about half an hour ago and bought some peppermints and talked a bit, and then went off towards the Heath. But a second after, one of them runs back into the shop and says, 'Have I left a parcel!' Well, I looked everywhere and couldn't see one; so he says, 'Never mind; but if it should turn up, please post it to this address,' and he left me the address and a shilling for my trouble. And sure enough, though I thought I'd looked everywhere, I found he'd left a brown paper parcel, so I posted it to the place he said. I can't remember the address now; it was somewhere in Westminster. But as the thing seemed so important, I thought perhaps the police had come about it."

"So they have," said Valentin shortly. "Is Hampstead Heath near here?"

"Straight on for fifteen

minutes," said the woman, "and you'll come right out on the open." Valentin sprang out of the shop and began to run. The other detectives followed him at a reluctant trot.

The street they threaded was so narrow and shut in by shadows that when they came out unexpectedly into the void common and vast sky they were startled to find the evening still so light and clear. A perfect dome of peacock-green sank into gold amid the blackening trees and the dark violet distances. The glowing green tint was just deep enough to pick out in points of crystal one or two stars. All that was left of the daylight lay in a golden glitter across the edge of Hampstead and that popular hollow which is called the Vale of Health. The holiday makers who roam this region had not wholly dispersed; a few couples sat shapelessly on benches; and here and there a distant girl still shrieked in one of the swings. The glory of heaven deepened and dark-ened around the sublime vulgarity of man; and standing on the slope and looking across the valley, Valentin be-held the thing which he sought.

Among the black and breaking groups in that dis-tance was one especially black which did not break—a group of two figures clerically clad. Though they seemed as small as insects, Valentin could see that one of them was much smaller than the other. Though the other had a student's stoop and an inconspicuous manner, he could see that the man was well over six feet high. He shut his teeth and went forward, whirling his stick impatiently. By the time he had substantially diminished the distance and magnified the two black figures as in a vast microscope, he had perceived something else; something which startled him, and yet which he had somehow expected. Whoever was the tall priest, there could be no doubt about the identity of the short one. It was his friend of the Harwich train, the stumpy little cure of Essex whom he had warned about his brown paper parcels.

Now, so far as this went, everything fitted in finally and rationally enough. Valentin had learned by his inquiries that morning that a Father Brown from Essex was bringing up a silver cross with sapphires, a relic of considerable value, to show some of the foreign priests at the congress. This undoubtedly was the "silver with blue stones"; and Father Brown undoubtedly was the little greenhorn in the train. Now there was nothing wonderful about the fact that what Valentin had found out Flambeau had also found out; Flambeau found out everything. Also there was nothing wonderful in the fact that when Flambeau heard of a sapphire cross he should try to steal it; that was the most natural thing in all natural history. And most certainly there was nothing wonderful about the fact that Flambeau should have it all his own way with such a silly sheep as the man with the umbrella and the parcels. He was the sort of man whom anybody could lead on a string to the North Pole; it was not surprising that an actor like Flambeau, dressed as another priest, could lead him to Hampstead Heath. So far the crime seemed clear enough; and while the detective pitied the priest for his helplessness, he almost despised Flambeau for condescending to so gullible a victim. But when Valentin thought of all that had happened in between, of all that had led him to his triumph, he racked his brains for the smallest rhyme or reason in it. What had the stealing of a blue-and-silver cross from a priest from Essex to do with chucking soup at wall paper? What had it to do with calling nuts oranges, or with paying for windows first and breaking them afterwards? He had come to the end of his chase; yet somehow he had missed the middle of it. When he failed (which was seldom), he had usually grasped the clue, but nevertheless missed the criminal. Here he had grasped the criminal, but still he could not grasp the clue.

The two figures that they followed were crawling like black flies across the huge green contour of a hill. They were evidently sunk in conversation, and perhaps did not notice where they were going; but they were certainly going to the wilder and more silent heights of the Heath. As their pursuers gained on them, the latter had to use the undignified attitudes of the deerstalker, to crouch behind clumps of trees and even to crawl prostrate in deep grass. By these ungainly ingenuities the hunters even came close enough to the quarry to hear the murmur of the discussion, but no word could be distinguished except the word "reason" recurring frequently in a high and almost childish voice. Once over an abrupt dip of land and a dense tangle of thickets, the detectives actually lost the two figures they were following. They did not find the trail again for an agonising ten minutes, and then it led round the brow of a great dome of hill overlooking an amphitheatre of rich and desolate sunset scenery. Under a tree in this commanding yet neglected spot was an old ramshackle wooden seat. On this seat sat the two priests still in serious speech together. The gorgeous green and gold still clung to the darkening horizon; but the dome above was turning slowly from peacock-green to peacock-blue, and the stars detached themselves more and more like solid jewels. Mutely motioning to his followers, Valentin contrived to creep up behind the big branching tree, and, standing there in deathly silence, heard the words of the strange priests for the first time.

After he had listened for a minute and a half, he was gripped by a devilish doubt. Perhaps he had dragged the two English policemen to the wastes of a nocturnal heath on an errand no saner than seeking figs on its thistles. For the two priests were talking exactly like priests, piously, with learning and leisure, about the most aerial enigmas of theology. The little Essex priest spoke the more simply, with his round face turned to the strengthening stars; the other talked with his head bowed, as if he were not even worthy to look at them. But no more innocently clerical conversation could have been heard in any white

Italian cloister or black Spanish cathedral.

The first he heard was the tail of one of Father Brown's sentences, which ended: "... what they really meant in the Middle Ages by the heavens being incorruptible."

The taller priest nodded his bowed head and said:

"Ah, yes, these modern infidels appeal to their reason; but who can look at those millions of worlds and not feel that there may well be wonderful universes above us where reason is utterly unreasonable?"

"No," said the other priest; "reason is always reasonable, even in the last limbo, in the lost borderland of things. I know that people charge the Church with lowering reason, but it is just the other way. Alone on earth, the Church makes reason really supreme. Alone on earth, the Church affirms that God himself is bound by reason."

The other priest raised his austere face to the spangled sky and said:

"Yet who knows if in that infinite universe—?"

"Only infinite physically," said the little priest, turning sharply in his seat, "not infinite in the sense of escaping from the laws of truth."

Valentin behind his tree was tearing his fingernails with silent fury. He seemed almost to hear the sniggers of the English detectives whom he had brought so far on a fantastic guess only to listen to the met- aphysical gossip of two mild old parsons. In his impatience he lost the equally elaborate answer of the tall cleric, and when he listened again it was again Father Brown who was speaking:

"Reason and justice grip the remotest and the loneliest star. Look at those stars. Don't they look as if they were single dia- monds and sapphires? Well, you can imagine any mad botany or geology you please. Think of forests of adamant with leaves of brilliants. Think the moon is a blue moon, a single elephantine sapphire. But don't fancy that all that frantic astronomy would make the smallest difference to the reason and justice of conduct. On plains of opal, under cliffs cut out of pearl, you would still find a notice-board, 'Thou shalt not steal.'"

Valentin was just in the act of rising from his rigid and

crouching attitude and creeping away as softly as might be, felled by the one great folly of his life. But something in the very silence of the tall priest made him stop until the latter spoke. When at last he did speak, he said simply, his head bowed and his hands on his knees:

"Well, I think that other worlds may perhaps rise higher than our reason. The mystery of heaven is unfathomable, and I for one can only bow my head."

Then, with brow yet bent and without changing by the faintest shade his attitude or voice, he added:

"Just hand over that sapphire cross of yours, will you? We're all alone here, and I could pull you to pieces like a straw doll."

The utterly unaltered voice and attitude added a strange violence to that shocking change of speech. But the guarder of the relic only seemed to turn his head by the smallest section of the compass. He seemed still to have a somewhat foolish face turned to the stars. Perhaps he had not understood. Or, perhaps, he had understood and sat rigid with terror.

"Yes," said the tall priest, in the same low voice and in the same still posture, "yes, I am Flambeau."

Then, after a pause, he said:

"Come, will you give me that cross?"

"No," said the other, and the monosyllable had an odd sound.

Flambeau suddenly flung off all his pontifical pretensions. The great robber leaned back in his seat and laughed low but long.

"No," he cried, "you won't give it me, you proud prelate. You won't give it me, you little celibate simpleton. Shall I tell you why you won't give it me? Because I've got it already in my own breast-pocket."

The small man from Essex turned what seemed to be a dazed face in the dusk, and said, with the timid eagerness of "The Private Secretary":

"Are—are you sure?"

Flambeau yelled with delight.

"Really, you're as good as a three-act farce," he cried. "Yes, you turnip, I am quite sure. I had the sense to make a duplicate of the right parcel, and now, my friend, you've got the duplicate and I've got the jewels. An old dodge, Father Brown—a very old dodge."

"Yes," said Father Brown, and passed his hand through his hair with the same strange vagueness of manner. "Yes, I've heard of it before."

The colossus of crime leaned over to the little rustic priest with a sort of sudden interest.

"You have heard of it?" he asked. "Where have you heard of it?"

"Well, I mustn't tell you his

name, of course," said the little man simply. "He was a penitent, you know. He had lived prosperously for about twenty years entirely on duplicate brown paper parcels. And so, you see, when I began to suspect you, I thought of this poor chap's way of doing it at once."

"Began to suspect me?" repeated the outlaw with increased intensity. "Did you really have the gumption to suspect me just because I brought you up to this bare part of the heath?"

"No, no," said Brown with an air of apology. "You see, I suspected you when we first met. It's that little bulge up the sleeve where you people have the spiked bracelet."

"How in Tartarus," cried Flambeau, "did you ever hear of the spiked bracelet?"

"Oh, one's little flock, you know!" said Father Brown, arching his eyebrows rather blankly. "When I was a curate in Hartlepool, there were three of them with spiked bracelets. So, as I suspected you from the first, don't you see, I made sure that the cross should go safe, anyhow. I'm afraid I watched you, you know. So at last I saw you change the parcels. Then, don't you see, I changed them back again. And then I left the right one behind."

"Left it behind?" repeated Flambeau, and for the first time there was another note in his voice beside his triumph.

"Well, it was like this," said the little priest, speaking in the same unaffected way. "I went back to that sweet-shop and asked if I'd left a parcel, and gave them a particular address if it turned up. Well, I knew I hadn't; but when I went away again I did. So, instead of running after me with that valuable parcel, they have sent it flying to a friend of mine in Westminster." Then he added rather sadly: "I learnt that, too, from a poor fellow in

Hartlepool. He used to do it with handbags he stole at railway stations, but he's in a monastery now. Oh, one gets to know, you know," he added, rubbing his head again with the same sort of desperate apology. "We can't help being priests. People come and tell us these things."

Flambeau tore a brown-paper parcel out of his inner pocket and rent it in pieces. There was nothing but paper and sticks of lead inside it. He sprang to his feet with a gigantic gesture, and cried:

"I don't believe you. I don't believe a bumpkin like you could manage all that. I believe you've still got the stuff on you, and if you don't give it up—why, we're all alone, and I'll take it by force!"

"No," said Father Brown simply, and stood up also, "you won't take it by force. First, because I really haven't still got it. And, second, because we are not alone."

Flambeau stopped in his stride forward.

"Behind that tree," said Father Brown, pointing, "are two strong policemen and the greatest detective alive. How did they come here, do you ask? Why, I brought them, of course! How did I do it? Why, I'll tell you if you like! Lord bless you, we have to know twenty such things when we work among the criminal classes! Well, I wasn't sure you were a thief, and it would never do to make a scandal against one of our own clergy. So I just tested you to see if anything would make you show yourself. A man generally makes a small scene if he finds salt in his coffee; if he doesn't, he has some reason for keeping quiet. I changed the salt and sugar, and you kept quiet. A man generally objects if his bill is three times too big. If he pays it, he has some motive for passing unnoticed. I altered your bill, and you paid it."

The world seemed waiting for Flambeau to leap like a tiger. But he was held back as by a spell; he was stunned with the utmost curiosity.

"Well," went on Father Brown, with lumbering lucidity, "as you wouldn't leave any tracks for the police, of course somebody had to. At every place we went to, I took care to do something that would get us talked about for the rest of the day. I didn't do much harm—a splashed wall, spilt apples, a broken window; but I saved the cross, as the cross will always be saved. It is at Westminster by now. I rather wonder you didn't stop it with the Donkey's Whistle."

"With the what?" asked Flambeau.

"I'm glad you've never heard of it," said the priest, making a face. "It's a foul thing. I'm sure you're too good a man for a Whistler. I couldn't have countered it even with the Spots myself; I'm not strong enough in the legs."

"What on earth are you talking about?" asked the other.

"Well, I did think you'd know the Spots," said Father Brown, agreeably surprised. "Oh, you can't have gone so very wrong yet!"

"How in blazes do you know all these horrors?" cried Flambeau.

The shadow of a smile crossed the round, simple face of his clerical opponent.

"Oh, by being a celibate

simpleton, I suppose," he said. "Has it never struck you that a man who does next to nothing but hear men's real sins is not likely to be wholly unaware of human evil? But, as a matter of fact, another part of my trade, too, made me sure you weren't a priest."

"What?" asked the thief, almost gaping.

"You attacked reason," said Father Brown. "It's bad theology."

And even as he turned

away to collect his property, the three policemen came out from under the twilight trees. Flambeau was an artist and a sportsman. He stepped back and swept Valentin a great bow.

"Do not bow to me, mon ami," said Valentin with silver clearness. "Let us both bow to our master."

And they both stood an instant uncovered while the little Essex priest blinked about for his umbrella.

The Secret Garden

Aristide Valentin, Chief of the Paris Police, was late for his dinner, and some of his guests began to arrive before him. These were, however, reassured by his confidential servant, Ivan, the old man with a scar, and a face almost as grey as his moustaches, who always sat at a table in the entrance hall—a hall hung with weapons. Valentin's house was perhaps as peculiar and celebrated as its master. It was an old house, with high walls and tall poplars almost over-hanging the Seine; but the oddity—and perhaps the po-lice value—of its architecture was this: that there was no ulti-mate exit at all except through this front door, which was guarded by Ivan and the ar-moury. The garden was large and elaborate, and there were many exits from the house into the garden. But there was no exit from the garden into the world outside; all round it ran a tall, smooth, unscalable wall with special spikes at the top; no bad garden, perhaps, for a man to reflect in whom some hundred criminals had sworn to kill.

As Ivan explained to the guests, their host had telephoned that he was detained for ten minutes. He was, in truth, making some last arrangements about executions and such ugly things; and though these duties were rootedly repulsive to him, he always performed them with precision. Ruthless in the pursuit of criminals, he was very mild about their punishment. Since he had been supreme over French—and largely over European—policial methods, his great influence had been honourably used for the mitigation of sentences and the purification of prisons. He was one of the great humanitarian French freethinkers; and the only thing wrong with them is that they make mercy even colder than justice.

When Valentin arrived he was already dressed in black clothes and the red rosette—an elegant figure, his dark beard already streaked with grey. He went straight through his house to his study, which opened on the grounds behind. The garden door of it was open, and after he had carefully locked his box in its official place, he stood for a few seconds at the open door looking out upon the garden. A sharp moon was fighting with the flying rags and tatters of a storm, and Valentin regarded it with a wistfulness unusual in such scientific natures as his. Perhaps such scientific natures have some psychic prevision of the most tremendous problem of their lives. From any such occult mood, at least, he quickly recovered, for he knew he was late, and that his guests had already begun to arrive. A glance at his drawing-room when he entered it was enough to make certain that his principal guest was not there, at any rate. He saw all the other pillars of the little party; he saw Lord Galloway, the English Ambassador—a choleric old man with a russet face like an apple, wearing the blue ribbon of the Garter. He saw Lady Galloway, slim and threadlike, with silver hair and a face sensitive and superior. He saw her daughter, Lady Margaret Graham, a pale and pretty girl with an elf-ish face and copper-coloured hair. He saw the Duchess of Mont St. Michel, black-eyed and opulent, and with her her two daughters, black-eyed and opulent also. He saw Dr. Simon, a typical French scientist, with glasses, a pointed brown beard, and a forehead barred with those parallel wrinkles which are the penalty of superciliousness, since they come through constantly elevating the eyebrows. He saw Father Brown, of Cobhole, in Essex, whom he had recently met in England. He saw—perhaps with more interest than any of these—a tall man in uniform, who had bowed to the Galloways without receiving any very hearty acknowledgment, and who now advanced alone to pay his respects to his host. This was Commandant O'Brien, of the French Foreign Legion. He was

a slim yet somewhat swaggering figure, clean-shaven, dark-
haired, and blue-eyed, and,
as seemed natural in an officer
of that famous regiment of vic-
torious failures and successful
suicides, he had an air at once
dashing and melancholy. He
was by birth an Irish gentleman, and in boyhood had
known the Galloways—espe-
cially Margaret Graham. He
had left his country after some
crash of debts, and now expressed his complete freedom

from British etiquette by swinging about in uniform, sabre and spurs. When he bowed to the Ambassador's family, Lord and Lady Galloway bent stiffly, and Lady Margaret looked away.

But for whatever old causes such people might be interested in each other, their distinguished host was not specially interested in them. No one of them at least was in his eyes the guest of the evening. Valentin was expecting, for special reasons, a man of world-wide fame, whose friendship he had secured during some of his great detective tours and triumphs in the United States. He was expecting Julius K. Brayne, that multi-millionaire whose colossal and even crushing endowments of small religions have occasioned so much easy sport and easier solemnity for the American and English papers. Nobody could quite make out whether Mr. Brayne was an atheist or a Mormon or a Christian Scientist; but he was ready to pour money into any intellectual vessel, so long as it was an untried vessel. One of his hobbies was to wait for the American Shakespeare—a hobby more patient than angling. He admired Walt Whitman, but thought that Luke P. Tanner, of Paris, Pa., was more "progressive" than Whitman any day. He liked anything that he thought "progressive." He thought

Valentin "progressive," thereby doing him a grave injustice.

The solid appearance of Julius K. Brayne in the room was as decisive as a dinner bell. He had this great quality, which very few of us can claim, that his presence was as big as his absence. He was a huge fellow, as fat as he was tall, clad in complete evening black, without so much relief as a watch-chain or a ring. His hair was white and well brushed back like a German's; his face was red, fierce and cherubic, with one dark tuft under the lower lip that threw up that otherwise infantile visage with an effect theatrical and even Mephistophelean. Not long, however, did that salon merely stare at the celebrated American; his lateness had already become a domestic problem, and he was sent with all speed into the dining-room with Lady Galloway on his arm.

Except on one point the Galloways were genial and

casual enough. So long as Lady Margaret did not take the arm of that adventurer O'Brien, her father was quite satisfied; and she had not done so, she had decorously gone in with Dr. Simon. Nevertheless, old Lord Galloway was restless and almost rude. He was diplomatic enough during dinner, but when, over the cigars, three of the younger men—Simon the doctor, Brown the priest, and the detrimental O'Brien, the exile in a foreign uniform—all melted away to mix with the ladies or smoke in the conservatory, then the English diplomatist grew very undiplomatic indeed. He was stung every sixty seconds with the thought that the scamp O'Brien might be signalling to Margaret somehow; he did not attempt to imagine how. He was left over the coffee with Brayne, the hoary Yankee who believed in all religions, and Valentin, the grizzled Frenchman who believed in none. They could argue with each other, but neither could appeal to him. After a time this "progressive" logomachy had reached a crisis of tedium; Lord Galloway got up also and sought the drawing-room. He lost his way in long passages for some six or eight minutes: till he heard the high-pitched, didactic voice of the doctor, and then the dull voice of the priest, followed by general laughter. They also, he thought with a curse, were probably arguing about "science and religion." But the instant he opened the salon door he saw only one thing—he saw what was not there. He saw that Commandant O'Brien was absent, and that Lady Margaret was absent too.

Rising impatiently from the drawing-room, as he had from the dining-room, he stamped along the passage once more. His notion of protecting his daughter from the Irish-

Algerian n'er-do-well had become something central and even mad in his mind. As he went towards the back of the house, where was Valentin's study, he was surprised to meet his daughter, who swept past with a white, scornful face, which was a second enigma. If she had been with O'Brien, where was O'Brien! If she had not been with O'Brien, where had she been? With a sort of senile and passionate suspicion he groped his way to the dark back parts of the mansion, and eventually found a servants' entrance that opened on to the garden. The moon with her scimitar had now ripped up and rolled away all the storm-wrack. The argent light lit up all four corners of the garden. A tall figure in blue was striding across the lawn towards the study door; a glint of moonlit silver on his facings picked him out as Commandant O'Brien.

He vanished through the

French windows into the house, leaving Lord Galloway in an indescribable temper, at once virulent and vague. The blue-and-silver garden, like a scene in a theatre, seemed to taunt him with all that tyrannic tenderness against which his worldly authority was at war. The length and grace of the Irishman's stride enraged him as if he were a rival instead of a father; the moonlight maddened him. He was trapped as if by magic into a garden of troubadours, a Watteau fairy-land; and, willing to shake off such amorous imbecilities by speech, he stepped briskly after his enemy. As he did so he tripped over some tree or stone in the grass; looked down at it first with irritation and then a second time with curiosity. The next instant the moon and the tall poplars looked at an unusual sight—an elderly English diplomatist running hard and crying or bellowing as he ran.

His hoarse shouts brought a pale face to the study door, the beaming glasses and worried brow of Dr. Simon, who heard the nobleman's first clear words. Lord Galloway was crying: "A corpse in the grass—a blood-stained corpse." O'Brien at last had gone utterly out of his mind.

"We must tell Valentin at once," said the doctor, when the other had brokenly described all that he had dared to examine. "It is fortunate that he is here;" and even as he spoke the great detective entered the study, attracted by the cry. It was almost amusing to note his typical transformation; he had come with the common concern of a host and a gentleman, fearing that some guest or servant was ill. When he was told the gory fact, he turned with all his gravity instantly bright and businesslike; for this, however abrupt and awful, was his business.

"Strange, gentlemen," he said as they hurried out into the garden, "that I should have hunted mysteries all over the earth, and now one comes and settles in my own back-yard. But where is the place?" They crossed the lawn less easily, as a slight mist had begun to rise from the river; but under the guidance of the shaken Galloway they found the body sunken in deep grass—the body of a very tall and broad-shouldered man.

He lay face downwards, so they could only see that his big shoulders were clad in black cloth, and that his big head was bald, except for a wisp or two of brown hair that clung to his skull like wet seaweed. A scarlet serpent of blood crawled from under his fallen face.

"At least," said Simon, with a deep and singular intonation, "he is none of our party."

"Examine him, doctor," cried Valentin rather sharply. "He

may not be dead."

The doctor bent down. "He is not quite cold, but I am afraid he is dead enough," he answered. "Just help me to lift him up."

They lifted him carefully an inch from the ground, and all doubts as to his being really dead were settled at once and frightfully. The head fell away. It had been entirely sundered from the body; whoever had cut his throat had managed to sever the neck as well. Even Valentin was slightly shocked. "He must have been as strong as a gorilla," he muttered.

Not without a shiver, though he was used to anatomical abortions, Dr. Simon lifted the head. It was slightly slashed about the neck and jaw, but the face was substantially unhurt. It was a ponderous, yellow face, at once sunken and swollen, with a hawk-like nose and heavy lids—a face of a wicked Roman emperor, with, perhaps, a distant touch of a Chinese emperor. All present seemed to look at it with the coldest eye of ignorance. Nothing else could be noted about the man except that, as they had lifted his body, they had seen underneath it the white gleam of a shirt-front defaced with a red gleam of blood. As Dr. Simon said, the man had never been of their party. But he might very well have been trying to join it, for he had come dressed for such an occasion.

Valentin went down on his hands and knees and examined with his closest professional attention the grass and ground for some twenty yards round the body, in which he was assisted less skillfully by the doctor, and quite vaguely by the English lord. Nothing rewarded their grovellings except a few twigs, snapped or chopped into very small lengths, which Valentin lifted for an instant's examination and then tossed away.

"Twigs," he said gravely; "twigs, and a total stranger with his head cut off; that is all there is on this lawn."

There was an almost creepy stillness, and then the un-nerved Galloway called out sharply:

"Who's that! Who's that over there by the garden wall!"

A small figure with a foolishly large head drew waveringly near them in the moonlit haze; looked for an instant like a goblin, but turned out to be the harmless little priest whom they had left in the drawing-room.

"I say," he said meekly, "there are no gates to this garden, do you know."

Valentin's black brows had come together somewhat crossly, as they did on principle at the sight of the cassock. But he was far too just a man to deny the relevance of the remark. "You are right," he said. "Before we find out how he came to be killed, we may have to find out how he came to be here. Now listen to me, gentlemen. If it can be done without prejudice to my position and duty, we shall all agree that certain distinguished names might well be kept out of this. There are ladies, gentlemen, and there is a foreign ambassador. If we must mark it down as a crime, then it must be followed up as a crime. But till then I can use my own discretion. I am the head of the police; I am so public that I can afford to be private. Please Heaven, I will clear everyone of my own guests before I call in my men to look for anybody else. Gentlemen, upon your honour, you will none of you leave the house till tomorrow at noon; there are bedrooms for all. Simon, I think you know where to find my man, Ivan, in the front hall; he is a confidential man. Tell him to leave another servant on guard and come to me at once. Lord Galloway, you are certainly the best person to tell the ladies what has happened, and prevent a panic. They also must stay. Father Brown and I will remain with the body."

When this spirit of the captain spoke in Valentin he was obeyed like a bugle. Dr. Simon went through to the armoury and routed out Ivan, the public detective's private detective. Galloway went to the drawing-room and told the terrible news tactfully enough, so that by the time the company assembled there the ladies were already startled and already soothed. Meanwhile the good priest and the good atheist stood at the head and foot of the dead man motionless in the moonlight, like symbolic statues of their two philosophies of death.

Ivan, the confidential man with the scar and the moustaches, came out of the house like a cannon ball, and came racing across the lawn to Valentin like a dog to his master. His livid face was quite lively with the glow of this domestic detective story, and it was with almost unpleasant eagerness that he asked his master's permission to examine the remains.

"Yes; look, if you like, Ivan," said Valentin, "but don't be long. We must go in and thrash this out in the house."

Ivan lifted the head, and

then almost let it drop.

"Why," he gasped, "it's—no, it isn't; it can't be. Do you know this man, sir?"

"No," said Valentin indifferently; "we had better go inside."

Between them they carried the corpse to a sofa in the study, and then all made their way to the drawing-room.

The detective sat down at a desk quietly, and even without hesitation; but his eye was the iron eye of a judge at assize.

He made a few rapid notes upon paper in front of him, and then said shortly: "Is everybody here?"

"Not Mr. Brayne," said the Duchess of Mont St. Michel, looking round.

"No," said Lord Galloway in a hoarse, harsh voice. "And not Mr. Neil O'Brien, I fancy. I saw that gentleman walking in the garden when the corpse was still warm."

"Ivan," said the detective, "go and fetch Commandant

O'Brien and Mr. Brayne. Mr. Brayne, I know, is finishing a cigar in the dining-room; Commandant O'Brien, I think, is walking up and down the conservatory. I am not sure."

The faithful attendant flashed from the room, and before anyone could stir or speak Valentin went on with the same soldierly swiftness of exposition.

"Everyone here knows that a dead man has been found in the garden, his head cut clean from his body. Dr. Simon, you have examined it. Do you think that to cut a man's throat like that would need great force? Or, perhaps, only a very sharp knife?"

"I should say that it could not be done with a knife at all," said the pale doctor.

"Have you any thought," resumed Valentin, "of a tool with which it could be done?"

"Speaking within modern probabilities, I really haven't," said the doctor, arching his painful brows. "It's not easy to hack a neck through even clumsily, and this was a very clean cut. It could be done with a battle-axe or an old headsman's axe, or an old two-handed sword."

"But, good heavens!" cried the Duchess, almost in hysterics, "there aren't any two-handed swords and battle-axes round here."

Valentin was still busy with the paper in front of him. "Tell me," he said, still writing rapidly, "could it have been done with a long French cavalry sabre?"

A low knocking came at the door, which, for some unreasonable reason, curdled everyone's blood like the knocking in Macbeth. Amid that frozen silence Dr. Simon managed to say: "A sabre— yes, I suppose it could."

"Thank you," said Valentin. "Come in, Ivan."

The confidential Ivan opened the door and ushered

in Commandant Neil O'Brien, whom he had found at last pacing the garden again.

The Irish officer stood up disordered and defiant on the threshold. "What do you want with me?" he cried.

"Please sit down," said Valentin in pleasant, level tones. "Why, you aren't wearing your sword. Where is it?"

"I left it on the library table," said O'Brien, his brogue deepening in his disturbed mood. "It was a nuisance, it was getting—"

"Ivan," said Valentin, "please go and get the Commandant's sword from the library." Then, as the servant vanished, "Lord Galloway says he saw you leaving the garden just before he found the corpse. What were you doing in the garden?"

The Commandant flung himself recklessly into a chair. "Oh," he cried in pure Irish, "admirin' the moon. Communing with Nature, me bhoy."

A heavy silence sank and endured, and at the end of it came again that trivial and terrible knocking. Ivan reappeared, carrying an empty steel scabbard. "This is all I can find," he said.

"Put it on the table," said Valentin, without looking up.

There was an inhuman silence in the room, like that sea of inhuman silence round the dock of the condemned murderer. The Duchess's weak exclamations had long ago died away. Lord Galloway's swollen hatred was satisfied and even sobered. The voice that came was quite unexpected.

"I think I can tell you," cried Lady Margaret, in that clear, quivering voice with which a courageous woman speaks publicly. "I can tell you what Mr. O'Brien was doing in the garden, since he is bound to silence. He was asking me to marry him. I refused; I said in my family circumstances I could give him nothing but my respect. He was a little angry at that; he did not seem to think much of my respect. I wonder," she added, with rather a wan smile, "if he will care at all for it now. For I offer it him now. I will swear anywhere that he never did a thing like this."

Lord Galloway had edged up to his daughter, and was intimidating her in what he imagined to be an undertone. "Hold your tongue, Maggie," he said in a thunderous whisper. "Why should you shield the fellow? Where's his sword? Where's his confounded cavalry—"

He stopped because of the singular stare with which his daughter was regarding him, a look that was indeed a lurid magnet for the whole group.

"You old fool!" she said in a low voice without pretence of piety, "what do you suppose you are trying to prove? I tell you this man was innocent while with me. But if he wasn't innocent, he was still with me. If he murdered a man in the garden, who was it who must have seen—who must at least have known? Do you hate Neil so much as to put your own daughter—"

Lady Galloway screamed. Everyone else sat tingling at the touch of those satanic tragedies that have been be-tween lovers before now. They saw the proud, white face of the Scotch aristocrat and her lover, the Irish adventurer, like old portraits in a dark house. The long silence was full of formless historical memories of murdered husbands and poisonous paramours.

In the centre of this morbid silence an innocent voice said: "Was it a very long cigar?"

The change of thought was so sharp that they had to look round to see who had spoken.

"I mean," said little Father Brown, from the corner of the room, "I mean that cigar Mr.

Brayne is finishing. It seems nearly as long as a walking-stick."

Despite the irrelevance there was assent as well as irritation in Valentin's face as he lifted his head.

"Quite right," he remarked sharply. "Ivan, go and see about Mr. Brayne again, and bring him here at once."

The instant the factotum had closed the door, Valentin addressed the girl with an entirely new earnestness.

"Lady Margaret," he said, "we all feel, I am sure, both gratitude and admiration for your act in rising above your lower dignity and explaining the Commandant's conduct. But there is a hiatus still. Lord Galloway, I understand, met you passing from the study to the drawing-room, and it was only some minutes afterwards that he found the garden and the Commandant still walking there."

"You have to remember,"

replied Margaret, with a faint irony in her voice, "that I had just refused him, so we should scarcely have come back arm in arm. He is a gentleman, anyhow; and he loitered behind—and so got charged with murder."

"In those few moments," said Valentin gravely, "he might really—"

The knock came again, and Ivan put in his scarred face.

"Beg pardon, sir," he said, "but Mr. Brayne has left the

house."

"Left!" cried Valentin, and rose for the first time to his feet.

"Gone. Scooted. Evaporated," replied Ivan in humorous French. "His hat and coat are gone, too, and I'll tell you something to cap it all. I ran outside the house to find any traces of him, and I found one, and a big trace, too."

"What do you mean?" asked Valentin.

"I'll show you," said his servant, and reappeared with a

156

flashing naked cavalry sabre, streaked with blood about the point and edge. Everyone in the room eyed it as if it were a thunderbolt; but the experienced Ivan went on quite quietly:

"I found this," he said, "flung among the bushes fifty yards up the road to Paris. In other words, I found it just where your respectable Mr. Brayne threw it when he ran away."

There was again a silence, but of a new sort. Valentin

took the sabre, examined it, reflected with unaffected concentration of thought, and then turned a respectful face to O'Brien. "Commandant," he said, "we trust you will always produce this weapon if it is wanted for police examination. Meanwhile," he added, slapping the steel back in the ringing scabbard, "let me return you your sword."

At the military symbolism of the action the audience could hardly refrain from applause.

For Neil O'Brien, indeed, that gesture was the turning-point of existence. By the time he was wandering in the mysterious garden again in the colours of the morning the tragic futility of his ordinary mien had fallen from him; he was a man with many reasons for happiness. Lord Galloway was a gentleman, and had offered him an apology. Lady Margaret was something better than a lady, a woman at least, and had perhaps given him something better than an apology, as they drifted among the old flowerbeds before breakfast. The whole company was more light-hearted and humane, for though the riddle of the death remained, the load of suspicion was lifted off them all, and sent flying off to Paris with the strange millionaire—a man they hardly knew. The devil was cast out of the house—he had cast himself out.

Still, the riddle remained;

and when O'Brien threw himself on a garden seat beside Dr. Simon, that keenly scientific person at once resumed it. He did not get much talk out of O'Brien, whose thoughts were on pleasanter things.

"I can't say it interests me much," said the Irishman frankly, "especially as it seems pretty plain now. Apparently Brayne hated this stranger for some reason; lured him into the garden, and killed him with my sword. Then he fled to the city, tossing the sword away as he went. By the way, Ivan tells me the dead man had a Yankee dollar in his pocket. So he was a countryman of Brayne's, and that seems to clinch it. I don't see any difficulties about the business."

"There are five colossal difficulties," said the doctor quietly; "like high walls within walls. Don't mistake me. I don't doubt that Brayne did it; his flight, I fancy, proves that. But as to how he did it. First difficulty: Why should a man kill another man with a great hulking sabre, when he can almost kill him with a pocket knife and put it back in his pocket? Second difficulty: Why was there no noise or outcry? Does a man commonly see another come up waving a scimitar and offer no remarks? Third difficulty: A servant watched the front door all the evening; and a rat cannot get into Valentin's garden anywhere. How did the dead man get into the garden? Fourth difficulty: Given the same conditions, how did Brayne get out of the garden?"

"And the fifth," said Neil, with eyes fixed on the English priest who was coming slowly up the path.

"Is a trifle, I suppose," said the doctor, "but I think an odd one. When I first saw how the head had been slashed, I supposed the assassin had struck more than once. But on examination I found many cuts across the truncated section; in other words, they were struck after the head was off. Did Brayne hate his foe so fiendishly that he stood sabring his body in the moonlight?"

"Horrible!" said O'Brien, and shuddered.

The little priest, Brown, had arrived while they were talking, and had waited, with characteristic shyness, till they had finished. Then he said awkwardly:

"I say, I'm sorry to interrupt.

But I was sent to tell you the news!"

"News?" repeated Simon, and stared at him rather painfully through his glasses.

"Yes, I'm sorry," said Father Brown mildly. "There's been another murder, you know."

Both men on the seat sprang up, leaving it rocking.

"And, what's stranger still," continued the priest, with his dull eye on the rhododendrons, "it's the same disgusting sort; it's another beheading.

They found the second head actually bleeding into the river, a few yards along Brayne's road to Paris; so they suppose that he—"

"Great Heaven!" cried O'Brien. "Is Brayne a monomaniac?"

"There are American vendettas," said the priest impassively. Then he added: "They want you to come to the library and see it."

Commandant O'Brien followed the others towards the

inquest, feeling decidedly sick. As a soldier, he loathed all this secretive carnage; where were these extravagant amputations going to stop? First one head was hacked off, and then another; in this case (he told himself bitterly) it was not true that two heads were better than one. As he crossed the study he almost staggered at a shocking coincidence. Upon Valentin's table lay the coloured picture of yet a third bleeding head; and it was the head of Valentin himself. A second glance showed him it was only a Nationalist paper, called *The Guillotine*, which every week showed one of its political opponents with rolling eyes and writhing features just after execution; for Valentin was an anti-clerical of some note. But O'Brien was an Irishman, with a kind of chastity even in his sins; and his gorge rose against that great brutality of the intellect which belongs only to France. He felt

Paris as a whole, from the grotesques on the Gothic churches to the gross caricatures in the newspapers. He remembered the gigantic jests of the Revolution. He saw the whole city as one ugly energy, from the sanguinary sketch lying on Valentin's table up to where, above a mountain and forest of gargoyles, the great devil grins on Notre Dame.

The library was long, low, and dark; what light entered it shot from under low blinds and had still some of the ruddy tinge of morning. Valentin and his servant Ivan were waiting for them at the upper end of a long, slightly-sloping desk, on which lay the mortal remains, looking enormous in the twilight. The big black figure and yellow face of the man found in the garden confronted them essentially unchanged. The second head, which had been fished from among the river reeds that morning, lay streaming and dripping beside it; Valentin's men were still seeking to recover the rest of this second corpse, which was supposed to be afloat. Father Brown, who did not seem to share O'Brien's sensibilities in the least, went up to the second head and examined it with his blinking care. It was little more than a mop of wet white hair, fringed with silver fire in the red and level morning light; the face, which seemed of an ugly, empurpled and perhaps criminal type, had been much battered against trees or stones as it tossed in the water.

"Good morning, Commandant O'Brien," said Valentin, with quiet cordiality. "You have heard of Brayne's last experiment in butchery, I suppose?"

Father Brown was still bending over the head with white hair, and he said, without looking up:

"I suppose it is quite certain that Brayne cut off this head, too."

"Well, it seems common sense," said Valentin, with his hands in his pockets. "Killed in the same way as the other. Found within a few yards of the other. And sliced by the same weapon which we know he carried away."

"Yes, yes; I know," replied Father Brown submissively. "Yet, you know, I doubt whether Brayne could have cut off this head."

"Why not?" inquired Dr.

Simon, with a rational stare.

"Well, doctor," said the priest, looking up blinking, "can a man cut off his own head? I don't know."

O'Brien felt an insane universe crashing about his ears; but the doctor sprang forward with impetuous practicality and pushed back the wet white hair.

"Oh, there's no doubt it's Brayne," said the priest quietly. "He had exactly that chip in the left ear."

The detective, who had been regarding the priest with steady and glittering eyes, opened his clenched mouth and said sharply: "You seem to know a lot about him, Father Brown."

"I do," said the little man simply. "I've been about with him for some weeks. He was thinking of joining our church."

The star of the fanatic sprang into Valentin's eyes; he strode towards the priest with clenched hands. "And, perhaps," he cried, with a blasting sneer, "perhaps he was also thinking of leaving all his money to your church."

"Perhaps he was," said Brown stolidly; "it is possible."

"In that case," cried Valentin, with a dreadful smile, "you may indeed know a great deal about him. About his life and about his—"

Commandant O'Brien laid a hand on Valentin's arm. "Drop that slanderous rubbish, Valentin," he said, "or there may be more swords yet."

But Valentin (under the steady, humble gaze of the priest) had already recovered himself. "Well," he said shortly, "people's private opinions can wait. You gentlemen are still bound by your promise to stay; you must enforce it on your-selves—and on each other. Ivan here will tell you anything more you want to know; I must get to business and write to the authorities. We can't keep this quiet any longer. I shall be writing in my study if there is any more news."

"Is there any more news, Ivan?" asked Dr. Simon, as the chief of police strode out of the room.

"Only one more thing, I think, sir," said Ivan, wrinkling up his grey old face, "but that's important, too, in its way. There's that old buffer you found on the lawn," and he pointed without pretence of reverence at the big black body with the yellow head.

"We've found out who he is, anyhow."

"Indeed!" cried the astonished doctor, "and who is he?"

"His name was Arnold Becker," said the under-detective, "though he went by many aliases. He was a wandering sort of scamp, and is known to have been in America; so that was where Brayne got his knife into him. We didn't have much to do with him ourselves, for he worked mostly in Germany. We've communicated, of course, with the German police. But, oddly enough, there was a twin brother of his, named Louis Becker, whom we had a great deal to do with. In fact, we found it necessary to guillotine him only yesterday. Well, it's a rum thing, gentlemen, but when I saw that fellow flat on the lawn I had the greatest jump of my life. If I hadn't seen Louis Becker guillotined with my own eyes, I'd have sworn it was Louis Becker lying there in the grass. Then, of course, I remembered his twin brother in Germany, and following up the clue—"

The explanatory Ivan stopped, for the excellent reason that nobody was listening to him. The Commandant and the doctor were both staring at Father Brown, who had sprung stiffly to his feet, and was holding his temples tight like a man in sudden and violent pain.

"Stop, stop, stop!" he cried;

"stop talking a minute, for I see half. Will God give me strength? Will my brain make the one jump and see all? Heaven help me! I used to be fairly good at thinking. I could paraphrase any page in Aquinas once. Will my head split— or will it see? I see half—I only see half."

He buried his head in his hands, and stood in a sort of rigid torture of thought or prayer, while the other three could only go on staring at this last prodigy of their wild twelve hours.

When Father Brown's hands fell they showed a face quite fresh and serious, like a child's. He heaved a huge sigh, and said: "Let us get this said and done with as quickly as possible. Look here, this will be the quickest way to convince you all of the truth." He turned to the doctor. "Dr. Simon," he said, "you have a strong headpiece, and I heard you this morning asking the five hardest questions about this business. Well, if you will ask them again, I will answer them."

Simon's pince-nez dropped from his nose in his doubt and wonder, but he answered at once. "Well, the first question, you know, is why a man should kill another with a clumsy sabre at all when a man can kill with a bodkin?"

"A man cannot behead with a bodkin," said Brown calmly, "and for this murder beheading was absolutely necessary."

"Why?" asked O'Brien, with interest.

"And the next question?" asked Father Brown.

"Well, why didn't the man cry out or anything?" asked the doctor; "sabres in gardens are certainly unusual."

"Twigs," said the priest gloomily, and turned to the window which looked on the scene of death. "No one saw the point of the twigs. Why should they lie on that lawn (look at it) so far from any tree? They were not snapped off; they were chopped off. The murderer occupied his enemy with some tricks with the sabre, showing how he could cut a branch in mid-air, or what-not. Then, while his enemy bent down to see the result, a silent slash, and the head fell."

"Well," said the doctor slowly, "that seems plausible enough. But my next two questions will stump anyone."

The priest still stood looking critically out of the window and waited.

"You know how all the garden was sealed up like an airtight chamber," went on the doctor. "Well, how did the strange man get into the garden?"

Without turning round, the little priest answered: "There never was any strange man in the garden."

There was a silence, and

then a sudden cackle of almost childish laughter relieved
the strain. The absurdity of
Brown's remark moved Ivan to
open taunts.

"Oh!" he cried; "then we
didn't lug a great fat corpse
on to a sofa last night? He
hadn't got into the garden, I
suppose?"

"Got into the garden?" repeated Brown reflectively.
"No, not entirely."

"Hang it all," cried Simon, "a
man gets into a garden, or he

doesn't."

"Not necessarily," said the priest, with a faint smile. "What is the nest question, doctor?"

"I fancy you're ill," exclaimed Dr. Simon sharply; "but I'll ask the next question if you like. How did Brayne get out of the garden?"

"He didn't get out of the garden," said the priest, still looking out of the window.

"Didn't get out of the garden?" exploded Simon.

"Not completely," said

Father Brown.

Simon shook his fists in a frenzy of French logic. "A man gets out of a garden, or he doesn't," he cried.

"Not always," said Father Brown.

Dr. Simon sprang to his feet impatiently. "I have no time to spare on such senseless talk," he cried angrily. "If you can't understand a man being on one side of a wall or the other, I won't trouble you further."

"Doctor," said the cleric very

gently, "we have always got on very pleasantly together. If only for the sake of old friendship, stop and tell me your fifth question."

The impatient Simon sank into a chair by the door and said briefly: "The head and shoulders were cut about in a queer way. It seemed to be done after death."

"Yes," said the motionless priest, "it was done so as to make you assume exactly the one simple falsehood that you did assume. It was done to make you take for granted that the head belonged to the body."

The borderland of the brain, where all the monsters are made, moved horribly in the Gaelic O'Brien. He felt the chaotic presence of all the horse-men and fish-women that man's unnatural fancy has begotten. A voice older than his first fathers seemed saying in his ear: "Keep out of the monstrous garden where grows the tree with double fruit. Avoid the evil garden where died the man with two heads." Yet, while these shameful symbolic shapes passed across the ancient mirror of his Irish soul, his Frenchified intellect was quite alert, and was watching the odd priest as closely and incredulously as all the rest.

Father Brown had turned round at last, and stood against the window, with his face in dense shadow; but even in that shadow they could see it was pale as ashes. Nevertheless, he spoke quite sensibly, as if there were no Gaelic souls on earth.

"Gentlemen," he said, "you did not find the strange body of Becker in the garden. You did not find any strange body in the garden. In face of Dr. Simon's rationalism, I still affirm that Becker was only partly present. Look here!" (pointing to the black bulk of the mysterious corpse) "you never saw that man in your lives. Did you ever see this man?"

He rapidly rolled away the bald, yellow head of the unknown, and put in its place the white-maned head beside it. And there, complete, unified, unmistakable, lay Julius K. Brayne.

"The murderer," went on Brown quietly, "hacked off his enemy's head and flung the sword far over the wall. But he was too clever to fling the sword only. He flung the head over the wall also. Then he had only to clap on another head to the corpse, and (as he insisted on a private inquest) you all imagined a totally new man."

"Clap on another head!" said O'Brien staring. "What other head? Heads don't grow on garden bushes, do they?"

"No," said Father Brown huskily, and looking at his boots; "there is only one place where they grow. They grow in the basket of the guillotine, beside which the chief of police, Aristide Valentin, was standing not an hour before the murder. Oh, my friends, hear me a minute more before you tear me in pieces. Valentin is an honest man, if being mad for an arguable cause is honesty. But did you never see in that cold, grey eye of his that he is mad! He would do anything, anything, to break what he calls the superstition of the Cross. He has fought for it and starved for it, and now he has murdered for it. Brayne's crazy millions had hitherto been scattered among so many sects that they did little to alter the balance of things. But Valentin heard a whisper that Brayne, like so many scatter-brained sceptics, was drifting to us; and that was quite a different thing. Brayne would pour supplies into the impoverished and pugnacious Church of France; he would support six Nationalist newspapers like *The*

Guillotine. The battle was already balanced on a point, and the fanatic took flame at the risk. He resolved to destroy the millionaire, and he did it as one would expect the greatest of detectives to commit his only crime. He abstracted the severed head of Becker on some criminological excuse, and took it home in his official box. He had that last argument with Brayne, that Lord Galloway did not hear the end of; that failing, he led him out into the sealed garden, talked about swordsmanship, used twigs and a sabre for illustration, and—"

Ivan of the Scar sprang up. "You lunatic," he yelled; "you'll go to my master now, if I take you by—"

"Why, I was going there," said Brown heavily; "I must ask him to confess, and all that."

Driving the unhappy Brown before them like a hostage or sacrifice, they rushed together into the sudden stillness of

Valentin's study.

The great detective sat at his desk apparently too occupied to hear their turbulent entrance. They paused a moment, and then something in the look of that upright and elegant back made the doctor run forward suddenly. A touch and a glance showed him that there was a small box of pills at Valentin's elbow, and that Valentin was dead in his chair; and on the blind face of the suicide was more than the pride of Cato.

The Queer Feet

If you meet a member of that select club, "The Twelve True Fishermen," entering the Vernon Hotel for the annual club dinner, you will observe, as he takes off his overcoat, that his evening coat is green and not black. If (supposing that you have the star-defying audacity to address such a being) you ask him why, he will probably answer that he does it to avoid being mistaken for a waiter. You will then retire crushed. But you will leave behind you a mystery as yet unsolved and a tale worth telling.

If (to pursue the same vein of improbable conjecture) you were to meet a mild, hard-working little priest, named Father Brown, and were to ask him what he thought was the most singular luck of his life, he would probably reply that upon the whole his best stroke was at the Vernon Hotel, where he had averted a crime and, perhaps, saved a soul, merely by listening to a few footsteps in a passage. He is perhaps a little proud of this wild and wonderful guess of his, and it is possible that he might refer to it. But since it is immeasurably unlikely that you will ever rise high enough in the social world to find "The

Twelve True Fishermen," or that you will ever sink low enough among slums and criminals to find Father Brown, I fear you will never hear the story at all unless you hear it from me.

The Vernon Hotel at which The Twelve True Fishermen held their annual dinners was an institution such as can only exist in an oligarchical society which has almost gone mad on good manners. It was that topsy-turvy product—an "exclusive" commercial enterprise. That is, it was a thing which paid not by at-tracting people, but actually by turning people away. In the heart of a plutocracy trades-men become cunning enough to be more fastidious than their customers. They positively create difficulties so that their wealthy and weary clients may spend money and diplo-macy in overcoming them. If there were a fashionable hotel in London which no man could enter who was under six foot, society would meekly make up parties of six-foot men to dine in it. If there were an expensive restaurant which by a mere caprice of its proprietor was only open on Thursday afternoon, it would be crowded on Thursday afternoon. The Vernon Hotel stood, as if by accident, in the corner of a square in Belgravia. It was a small hotel; and a very inconvenient one. But its very inconveniences were considered as walls protecting a particular class. One inconvenience, in particular, was held to be of vital importance: the fact that practically only twenty-four people could dine in the place at once. The only big dinner table was the celebrated terrace table, which stood open to the air on a sort of veranda overlooking one of the most exquisite old gardens in London. Thus it happened that even the twenty-four seats at this table could only be enjoyed in warm weather;

and this making the enjoyment yet more difficult made it yet more desired. The existing owner of the hotel was a Jew named Lever; and he made nearly a million out of it, by making it difficult to get into. Of course he combined with this limitation in the scope of his enterprise the most careful polish in its performance. The wines and cooking were really as good as any in Europe, and the demeanour of the attendants exactly mirrored the fixed mood of the English upper class. The proprietor knew all his waiters like the fingers on his hand; there were only fifteen of them all told. It was much easier to become a Member of Parliament than to become a waiter in that hotel. Each waiter was trained in terrible silence and smoothness, as if he were a gentleman's servant. And, indeed, there was generally at least one waiter to every gentleman who dined.

The club of The Twelve True

Fishermen would not have consented to dine anywhere but in such a place, for it insisted on a luxurious privacy; and would have been quite upset by the mere thought that any other club was even dining in the same building. On the occasion of their annual dinner the Fishermen were in the habit of exposing all their treasures, as if they were in a private house, especially the celebrated set of fish knives and forks which were, as it were, the insignia of the society, each being exquisitely wrought in silver in the form of a fish, and each loaded at the hilt with one large pearl. These were always laid out for the fish course, and the fish course was always the most magnificent in that magnificent repast. The society had a vast number of ceremonies and observances, but it had no history and no object; that was where it was so very aristocratic. You did not have to be anything in order to be one of the Twelve Fishers; unless you were already a certain sort of person, you never even heard of them. It had been in exist- ence twelve years. Its president was Mr. Audley. Its vice-president was the Duke of Chester.

If I have in any degree con- veyed the atmosphere of this appalling hotel, the reader may feel a natural wonder as to how I came to know any- thing about it, and may even speculate as to how so ordinary a person as my friend Father Brown came to find himself in that golden galley. As far as that is concerned, my story is simple, or even vulgar. There is in the world a very aged rioter and demagogue who breaks into the most refined retreats with the dreadful information that all men are brothers, and wherever this leveller went on his pale horse it was Father Brown's trade to follow. One of the waiters, an

Italian, had been struck down with a paralytic stroke that afternoon; and his Jewish employer, marvelling mildly at such superstitions, had consented to send for the nearest Popish priest. With what the waiter confessed to Father Brown we are not concerned, for the excellent reason that that cleric kept it to himself; but apparently it involved him in writing out a note or statement for the conveying of some message or the righting of some wrong. Father Brown, therefore, with a meek impudence which he would have shown equally in Buckingham Palace, asked to be provided with a room and writing materials. Mr. Lever was torn in two. He was a kind man, and had also that bad imitation of kindness, the dislike of any difficulty or scene. At the same time the presence of one unusual stranger in his hotel that evening was like a speck of dirt on something just cleaned. There was never any borderland or anteroom in the Vernon Hotel, no people waiting in the hall, no customers coming in on chance. There were fifteen waiters. There were twelve guests. It would be as startling to find a new guest in the hotel that night as to find a new brother taking breakfast or tea in one's own family. Moreover, the priest's appearance was second-rate and his clothes muddy; a mere glimpse of him afar off might precipitate a crisis in the club. Mr. Lever at last hit on a plan to cover, since he might not obliterate, the disgrace. When you enter (as you never will) the Vernon Hotel, you pass down a short passage decorated with a few dingy but important pictures, and come to the main vestibule and lounge which opens on your right into passages leading to the public rooms, and on your left to a similar passage pointing to the kitchens and offices of the hotel.

Immediately on your left hand is the corner of a glass office, which abuts upon the lounge—a house within a house, so to speak, like the old hotel bar which probably once occupied its place.

In this office sat the representative of the proprietor (nobody in this place ever appeared in person if he could help it), and just beyond the office, on the way to the servants' quarters, was the gentlemen's cloak room, the last boundary of the gentlemen's domain. But between the office and the cloak room was a small private room without other outlet, sometimes used by the proprietor for delicate and important matters, such as lending a duke a thousand pounds or declining to lend him sixpence. It is a mark of the magnificent tolerance of Mr. Lever that he permitted this holy place to be for about half an hour profaned by a mere priest, scribbling away on a piece of paper. The story which Father Brown was writing down was very likely a much better story than this one, only it will never be known. I can merely state that it was very nearly as long, and that the last two or three paragraphs of it were the least exciting and absorbing.

For it was by the time that he had reached these that the priest began a little to allow his thoughts to wander and his animal senses, which were commonly keen, to awaken. The time of darkness and dinner was drawing on; his own forgotten little room was without a light, and perhaps the gathering gloom, as occasionally happens, sharpened the sense of sound. As Father Brown wrote the last and least essential part of his document, he caught himself writing to the rhythm of a recurrent noise outside, just as one sometimes thinks to the tune of a railway train. When he became conscious of the thing he found what it was: only the ordinary patter of feet passing the door, which in an hotel was no very unlikely matter. Nevertheless, he stared at the darkened ceiling, and listened to the sound. After he had listened for a few seconds dreamily, he got to his feet and listened intently, with his head a little on one side. Then he sat down again and buried his brow in his hands, now not merely listening, but listening and thinking also.

The footsteps outside at any given moment were such as one might hear in any hotel; and yet, taken as a whole, there was something very strange about them. There were no other footsteps. It was always a very silent house, for the few familiar guests went at once to their own apartments, and the well-trained waiters were told to be almost invisible until they were wanted. One could not conceive any place where there was less reason to apprehend anything irregular. But these footsteps were so odd that one could not decide to call them regular or irregular. Father Brown followed them with his finger on the edge of the table, like a man trying to learn a tune on the piano.

First, there came a long rush of rapid little steps, such as a light man might make in winning a walking race. At a certain point they stopped and changed to a sort of slow, swinging stamp, numbering not a quarter of the steps, but occupying about the same time. The moment the last echoing stamp had died away would come again the run or ripple of light, hurrying feet, and then again the thud of the heavier walking. It was certainly the same pair of boots, partly because (as has been said) there were no other boots about, and partly because they had a small but unmistakable creak in them. Father Brown had the kind of head that cannot help asking questions; and on this apparently trivial question his head almost split. He had seen men run in order to jump. He had seen men run in order to slide. But why on earth should a man run in order to walk? Or, again, why should he walk in order to run? Yet no other description would cover the antics of this invisible pair of legs. The man was either walking very fast down one-half of the corridor in order to walk very slow down the other half; or he was walking very slow at one end to have the rapture of walking fast at the other. Neither suggestion seemed to make much sense. His brain was growing darker and darker, like his room.

Yet, as he began to think steadily, the very blackness of his cell seemed to make his thoughts more vivid; he began to see as in a kind of vision the fantastic feet capering along the corridor in unnatural or symbolic attitudes. Was it a heathen religious dance? Or some entirely new kind of scientific exercise? Father Brown began to ask himself with more exactness what the steps suggested. Taking the slow step first: it certainly was not the step of the proprietor. Men of his type walk with a rapid waddle, or they sit still. It could not be any servant or messenger waiting for directions. It did not sound like it. The poorer orders (in an oligarchy) sometimes lurch about when they are slightly drunk, but generally, and especially in such gorgeous scenes, they stand or sit in constrained attitudes. No; that heavy yet springy step, with a kind of careless emphasis, not specially noisy, yet not caring what noise it made, belonged to only one of the animals of this earth. It was a gentleman of western Europe, and probably one who had never worked for his living.

Just as he came to this solid certainty, the step changed to the quicker one, and ran past the door as feverishly as a rat. The listener remarked that though this step was much swifter it was also much more noiseless, almost as if the man were walking on tiptoe. Yet it was not associated in his mind with secrecy, but with something else—something that he could not remember. He was maddened by one of those half-memories that make a man feel half-witted. Surely he had heard that strange, swift walking somewhere. Suddenly he sprang to his feet with a new idea in his head, and walked to the door. His room had no direct outlet on the passage, but let on one side into the glass office, and on the other into the cloak room beyond. He tried the door into the office, and found it locked. Then he looked at the window,

now a square pane full of pur-
ple cloud cleft by livid sunset,
and for an instant he smelt evil
as a dog smells rats.

The rational part of him
(whether the wiser or not) re-
gained its supremacy. He
remembered that the proprietor had told him that he should
lock the door, and would
come later to release him. He
told himself that twenty things
he had not thought of might
explain the eccentric sounds
outside; he reminded himself

234

that there was just enough light left to finish his own proper work. Bringing his paper to the window so as to catch the last stormy evening light, he resolutely plunged once more into the almost completed record. He had written for about twenty minutes, bending closer and closer to his paper in the lessening light; then suddenly he sat upright. He had heard the strange feet once more.

This time they had a third

oddity. Previously the unknown man had walked, with levity indeed and lightning quickness, but he had walked. This time he ran. One could hear the swift, soft, bounding steps coming along the corridor, like the pads of a fleeing and leaping panther. Whoever was coming was a very strong, active man, in still yet tearing excitement. Yet, when the sound had swept up to the office like a sort of whispering whirlwind, it suddenly changed again to the old slow, swaggering stamp.

Father Brown flung down his paper, and, knowing the office door to be locked, went at once into the cloak room on the other side. The attendant of this place was temporarily absent, probably because the only guests were at dinner and his office was a sinecure. After groping through a grey forest of overcoats, he found that the dim cloak room opened on the lighted corridor in the form of a sort of counter or half-door, like most of the counters across which we have all handed umbrellas and received tickets. There was a light immediately above the semicircular arch of this opening. It threw little illumination on Father Brown himself, who seemed a mere dark outline against the dim sunset window behind him. But it threw an almost theatrical light on the man who stood outside the cloak room in the corridor.

He was an elegant man in very plain evening dress; tall, but with an air of not taking up much room; one felt that he could have slid along like a shadow where many smaller men would have been obvious and obstructive. His face, now flung back in the lamplight, was swarthy and vivacious, the face of a foreigner. His figure was good, his manners good humoured and confident; a critic could only say that his black coat was a shade below his figure and manners, and even bulged and bagged in an odd way. The moment he caught sight of Brown's black silhouette against the sunset, he tossed down a scrap of paper with a number and called out with amiable authority: "I want my hat and coat, please; I find I have to go away at once."

Father Brown took the paper without a word, and obediently went to look for the coat; it was not the first menial work he had done in his life. He brought it and laid it on the counter; meanwhile, the strange gentleman who had been feeling in his waistcoat pocket, said laughing: "I haven't got any silver; you can keep this." And he threw down half a sovereign, and caught up his coat.

Father Brown's figure remained quite dark and still; but in that instant he had lost his head. His head was always most valuable when he had lost it. In such moments he put two and two together and made four million. Often the Catholic Church (which is wedded to common sense) did not approve of it. Often he did not approve of it himself. But it was real inspiration—important at rare crises—when whosoever shall lose his head the same shall save it.

"I think, sir," he said civilly, "that you have some silver in your pocket."

The tall gentleman stared. "Hang it," he cried, "if I choose to give you gold, why should you complain?"

"Because silver is sometimes more valuable than gold," said the priest mildly; "that is, in large quantities."

The stranger looked at him curiously. Then he looked still more curiously up the passage towards the main entrance. Then he looked back at Brown again, and then he looked very carefully at the window beyond Brown's head, still coloured with the after-glow of the storm. Then he seemed to make up his mind. He put one hand on the counter, vaulted over as easily as an acrobat and towered above the priest, putting one tremendous hand upon his collar.

"Stand still," he said, in a hacking whisper. "I don't want to threaten you, but—"

"I do want to threaten you," said Father Brown, in a voice like a rolling drum, "I want to threaten you with the worm that dieth not, and the fire that is not quenched."

"You're a rum sort of cloak-room clerk," said the other.

"I am a priest, Monsieur Flambeau," said Brown, "and I am ready to hear your confession."

The other stood gasping for a few moments, and then staggered back into a chair.

The first two courses of the dinner of The Twelve True Fishermen had proceeded with placid success. I do not possess a copy of the menu; and if I did it would not convey anything to anybody. It was written in a sort of super-French employed by cooks, but quite unintelligible to Frenchmen. There was a tradition in the club that the *hors d'œuvres* should be various and manifold to the point of madness. They were taken seriously because they were avowedly useless extras, like the whole dinner and the whole club. There was also a tradition that the soup course should be light and unpretending—a sort of simple and austere vigil for the feast of fish that was to come. The talk was that strange, slight talk which governs the British Empire, which governs it in secret, and yet would scarcely enlighten an ordinary Englishman even if he could overhear it. Cabinet ministers on both sides were alluded to by their Christian names with a sort of bored benignity. The Radical Chancellor of the Exchequer, whom the whole Tory party was supposed to be cursing for his extortions, was praised for his minor poetry, or his saddle in the hunting field. The Tory leader, whom all Liberals were supposed to hate as a tyrant, was discussed and, on the whole, praised—as a Liberal. It seemed somehow that politicians were very important. And yet, anything seemed important about them except their politics. Mr. Audley, the chairman, was an amiable, elderly man who still wore Gladstone collars; he was a kind of symbol of all that phantasmal and yet fixed society. He had never done anything—not even anything wrong. He was not fast; he was not even particularly rich. He was simply in the thing; and there was an end of it. No party could ignore him, and if he had wished to be in the Cabinet he certainly would have been put there. The Duke of Chester, the vice-president, was a young and rising politician. That is to say, he was a pleasant youth, with flat, fair hair and a freckled face, with moderate intelligence and enormous estates. In public his appearances were always successful and his principle was simple enough. When he thought of a joke he made it, and was called brilliant. When he could not think of a joke he said that this was no time for trifling, and was called able. In private, in a club of his own class, he was simply quite pleasantly frank and silly, like a schoolboy. Mr. Audley, never having been in politics, treated them a little more seriously. Sometimes he even embarrassed the company by phrases suggesting that there was some difference between a Liberal and a Conservative. He himself was a Conservative, even in private life. He had a roll of grey hair over the back of his collar, like certain old-fashioned statesmen, and seen from behind he looked like the man the empire wants. Seen from the front he looked like a mild, self-indulgent bachelor, with rooms in the Albany—which he was.

As has been remarked, there were twenty-four seats at the terrace table, and only twelve members of the club. Thus they could occupy the terrace in the most luxurious style of all, being ranged along the inner side of the table, with no one opposite, commanding an uninterrupted view of the garden, the colours of which were still vivid, though evening was closing in somewhat luridly for the time of year. The chairman sat in the centre of the line, and the vice-president at the right-hand end of it. When the twelve guests first trooped into their seats it was the custom (for some unknown reason) for all the fifteen waiters to stand

lining the wall like troops pre-
senting arms to the king, while
the fat proprietor stood and
bowed to the club with radi-
ant surprise, as if he had never
heard of them before. But before the first chink of knife and
fork this army of retainers had
vanished, only the one or two
required to collect and distrib-
ute the plates darting about in
deathly silence. Mr. Lever, the
proprietor, of course had dis-
appeared in convulsions of
courtesy long before. It would

be exaggerative, indeed irrev-
erent, to say that he ever
positively appeared again. But
when the important course,
the fish course, was being
brought on, there was—how
shall I put it?—a vivid shadow,
a projection of his personality,
which told that he was hover-
ing near. The sacred fish
course consisted (to the eyes
of the vulgar) in a sort of monstrous pudding, about the size
and shape of a wedding
cake, in which some

considerable number of interesting fishes had finally lost the
shapes which God had given
to them. The Twelve True Fishermen took up their
celebrated fish knives and fish
forks, and approached it as
gravely as if every inch of the
pudding cost as much as the
silver fork it was eaten with. So
it did, for all I know. This course
was dealt with in eager and
devouring silence; and it was
only when his plate was nearly
empty that the young duke

made the ritual remark: "They can't do this anywhere but here."

"Nowhere," said Mr. Audley, in a deep bass voice, turning to the speaker and nodding his venerable head a number of times. "Nowhere, assuredly, except here. It was represented to me that at the Café Anglais—"

Here he was interrupted and even agitated for a moment by the removal of his plate, but he recaptured the valuable thread of his thoughts. "It was represented to me that the same could be done at the Café Anglais. Nothing like it, sir," he said, shaking his head ruthlessly, like a hanging judge. "Nothing like it."

"Overrated place," said a certain Colonel Pound, speaking (by the look of him) for the first time for some months.

"Oh, I don't know," said the Duke of Chester, who was an optimist, "it's jolly good for some things. You can't beat it at—"

A waiter came swiftly along the room, and then stopped dead. His stoppage was as silent as his tread; but all those vague and kindly gentlemen were so used to the utter smoothness of the unseen machinery which surrounded and supported their lives, that a waiter doing anything unexpected was a start and a jar. They felt as you and I would feel if the inanimate world disobeyed—if a chair ran away from us.

The waiter stood staring a few seconds, while there deepened on every face at table a strange shame which is wholly the product of our time. It is the combination of modern humanitarianism with the horrible modern abyss between the souls of the rich and poor. A genuine historic aristocrat would have thrown things at the waiter, beginning with empty bottles, and very probably ending with money. A genuine democrat would have asked him, with comrade-like clearness of speech, what the devil he was doing. But these modern plutocrats could not bear a poor man near to them, either as a slave or as a friend. That something had gone wrong with the servants was merely a dull, hot embarrassment. They did not want to be brutal, and they dreaded the need to be benevolent. They wanted the thing, whatever it was, to be over. It was over. The waiter, after standing for some seconds rigid, like a cataleptic, turned round and ran madly out of the room.

When he reappeared in the room, or rather in the doorway, it was in company with another waiter, with whom he whispered and gesticulated with southern fierceness. Then the first waiter went away, leaving the second waiter, and reappeared with a third waiter. By the time a fourth waiter had joined this hurried synod, Mr. Audley felt it necessary to break the silence in the interests of Tact. He used a very loud cough, instead of a presidential hammer, and said: "Splendid work young Moocher's doing in Burmah. Now, no other nation in the world could have—"

A fifth waiter had sped towards him like an arrow, and was whispering in his ear: "So sorry. Important! Might the proprietor speak to you?"

The chairman turned in disorder, and with a dazed stare saw Mr. Lever coming towards them with his lumbering quickness. The gait of the good proprietor was indeed his usual gait, but his face was by no means usual. Generally it was a genial copper-brown; now it was a sickly yellow.

"You will pardon me, Mr. Audley," he said, with asthmatic breathlessness. "I have great apprehensions. Your fish-plates, they are cleared away with the knife and fork on them!"

"Well, I hope so," said the chairman, with some warmth.

"You see him?" panted the excited hotel keeper; "you see the waiter who took them away? You know him?"

"Know the waiter?" answered Mr. Audley indignantly. "Certainly not!"

Mr. Lever opened his hands with a gesture of agony. "I never send him," he said. "I know not when or why he come. I send my waiter to take away the plates, and he find them already away."

Mr. Audley still looked rather too bewildered to be really the man the empire wants; none of the company could say anything except the man of wood—Colonel Pound—who seemed galvanised into an unnatural life. He rose rigidly from his chair, leaving all the rest sitting, screwed his eyeglass into his eye, and spoke in a raucous undertone as if he had half-forgotten how to speak. "Do you mean," he said, "that somebody has stolen our silver fish service?"

The proprietor repeated the open-handed gesture with even greater helplessness and in a flash all the men at the table were on their feet.

"Are all your waiters here?" demanded the colonel, in his low, harsh accent.

"Yes; they're all here. I noticed it myself," cried the

young duke, pushing his boyish face into the inmost ring. "Always count 'em as I come in; they look so queer standing up against the wall."

"But surely one cannot exactly remember," began Mr. Audley, with heavy hesitation.

"I remember exactly, I tell you," cried the duke excitedly. "There never have been more than fifteen waiters at this place, and there were no more than fifteen tonight, I'll swear; no more and no less."

The proprietor turned upon him, quaking in a kind of palsy of surprise. "You say—you say," he stammered, "that you see all my fifteen waiters?"

"As usual," assented the duke. "What is the matter with that!"

"Nothing," said Lever, with a deepening accent, "only you did not. For one of zem is dead upstairs."

There was a shocking stillness for an instant in that room. It may be (so supernatural is

269

the word death) that each of those idle men looked for a second at his soul, and saw it as a small dried pea. One of them—the duke, I think—even said with the idiotic kindness of wealth: "Is there anything we can do?"

"He has had a priest," said the Jew, not untouched.

Then, as to the clang of doom, they awoke to their own position. For a few weird seconds they had really felt as if the fifteenth waiter might be

270

the ghost of the dead man upstairs. They had been dumb under that oppression, for ghosts were to them an embarrassment, like beggars. But the remembrance of the silver broke the spell of the miraculous; broke it abruptly and with a brutal reaction. The colonel flung over his chair and strode to the door. "If there was a fifteenth man here, friends," he said, "that fifteenth fellow was a thief. Down at once to the front and back doors and secure everything; then we'll talk. The twenty-four pearls of the club are worth recovering."

Mr. Audley seemed at first to hesitate about whether it was gentlemanly to be in such a hurry about anything; but, seeing the duke dash down the stairs with youthful energy, he followed with a more mature motion.

At the same instant a sixth waiter ran into the room, and declared that he had found the pile of fish plates on a side-board, with no trace of the silver.

The crowd of diners and attendants that tumbled helter-skelter down the passages divided into two groups. Most of the Fishermen followed the proprietor to the front room to demand news of any exit. Colonel Pound, with the chairman, the vice-president, and one or two others darted down the corridor leading to the servants' quarters, as the more likely line of escape. As they did so they passed the dim alcove or cavern of the cloak room, and saw a short, black-coated figure, presumably an attendant, standing a little way back in the shadow of it.

"Hallo, there!" called out the duke. "Have you seen any-one pass?"

The short figure did not an-swer the question directly, but merely said: "Perhaps I have got what you are looking for, gentlemen."

They paused, wavering and wondering, while he quietly went to the back of the cloak room, and came back with both hands full of shining silver, which he laid out on the counter as calmly as a salesman. It took the form of a dozen quaintly shaped forks and knives.

"You—you—" began the colonel, quite thrown off his balance at last. Then he peered into the dim little room and saw two things: first, that the short, black-clad man was dressed like a clergyman; and, second, that the window of the room behind him was burst, as if someone had passed violently through. "Valuable things to deposit in a cloak room, aren't they?" remarked the clergyman, with cheerful composure.

"Did—did you steal those things?" stammered Mr. Audley, with staring eyes.

"If I did," said the cleric

pleasantly, "at least I am bringing them back again."

"But you didn't," said Colonel Pound, still staring at the broken window.

"To make a clean breast of it, I didn't," said the other, with some humour. And he seated himself quite gravely on a stool. "But you know who did," said the, colonel.

"I don't know his real name," said the priest placidly, "but I know something of his fighting weight, and a great deal about his spiritual difficulties. I formed the physical estimate when he was trying to throttle me, and the moral estimate when he repented."

"Oh, I say—repented!" cried young Chester, with a sort of crow of laughter.

Father Brown got to his feet, putting his hands behind him. "Odd, isn't it," he said, "that a thief and a vagabond should repent, when so many who are rich and secure remain hard and frivolous, and without fruit for God or man? But there, if you will excuse me, you trespass a little upon my province. If you doubt the penitence as a practical fact, there are your knives and forks. You are The Twelve True Fishers, and there are all your silver fish. But He has made me a fisher of men."

"Did you catch this man?" asked the colonel, frowning.

Father Brown looked him full in his frowning face. "Yes," he said, "I caught him, with an unseen hook and an invisible line which is long enough to let him wander to the ends of the world, and still to bring him back with a twitch upon the thread."

There was a long silence. All the other men present drifted away to carry the recovered silver to their comrades, or to consult the proprietor about the queer condition of affairs. But the grim-faced colonel still sat sideways on the counter, swinging his long, lank legs and biting his dark moustache.

At last he said quietly to the priest: "He must have been a clever fellow, but I think I know a cleverer."

"He was a clever fellow," answered the other, "but I am not quite sure of what other you mean."

"I mean you," said the colonel, with a short laugh. "I don't want to get the fellow jailed; make yourself easy about that. But I'd give a good many silver forks to know exactly how you fell into this affair, and how you got the stuff out of him. I reckon you're the most up-to-date devil of the present company."

Father Brown seemed rather to like the saturnine candour of the soldier. "Well," he said, smiling, "I mustn't tell you anything of the man's identity, or his own story, of course; but there's no particular reason why I shouldn't tell you of the mere outside facts which I found out for myself."

He hopped over the barrier with unexpected activity, and sat beside Colonel Pound, kicking his short legs like a little boy on a gate. He began to tell the story as easily as if he were telling it to an old friend by a Christmas fire.

"You see, colonel," he said, "I was shut up in that small room there doing some writing, when I heard a pair of feet in this passage doing a dance that was as queer as the dance of death. First came quick, funny little steps, like a man walking on tiptoe for a wager; then came slow, careless, creaking steps, as of a big man walking about with a cigar. But they were both made by the same feet, I swear, and they came in rotation; first the run and then the walk, and then the run again. I wondered at first idly and then wildly why a man should act these two parts at once. One walk I knew; it was just like yours, colonel. It was the walk

of a well-fed gentleman waiting for something, who strolls
about rather because he is
physically alert than because
he is mentally impatient. I
knew that I knew the other
walk, too, but I could not remember what it was. What
wild creature had I met on my
travels that tore along on tiptoe in that extraordinary style?
Then I heard a clink of plates
somewhere; and the answer
stood up as plain as St. Peter's.
It was the walk of a waiter—

that walk with the body slanted forward, the eyes looking down, the ball of the toe spurning away the ground, the coat tails and napkin flying. Then I thought for a minute and a half more. And I believe I saw the manner of the crime, as clearly as if I were going to commit it."

Colonel Pound looked at him keenly, but the speaker's mild grey eyes were fixed upon the ceiling with almost empty wistfulness.

"A crime," he said slowly, "is like any other work of art. Don't look surprised; crimes are by no means the only works of art that come from an infernal workshop. But every work of art, divine or diabolic, has one indispensable mark—I mean, that the centre of it is simple, however much the fulfilment may be complicated. Thus, in *Hamlet*, let us say, the grotesqueness of the gravedigger, the flowers of the mad girl, the fantastic finery of

Osric, the pallor of the ghost and the grin of the skull are all oddities in a sort of tangled wreath round one plain tragic figure of a man in black. Well, this also," he said, getting slowly down from his seat with a smile, "this also is the plain tragedy of a man in black. Yes," he went on, seeing the colonel look up in some wonder, "the whole of this tale turns on a black coat. In this, as in *Hamlet*, there are the rococo excrescences—

yourselves, let us say. There is the dead waiter, who was there when he could not be there. There is the invisible hand that swept your table clear of silver and melted into air. But every clever crime is founded ultimately on some one quite simple fact—some fact that is not itself mysterious. The mystification comes in covering it up, in leading men's thoughts away from it. This large and subtle and (in the ordinary course) most profitable crime, was built on the plain fact that a gentleman's evening dress is the same as a waiter's. All the rest was acting, and thundering good acting, too."

"Still," said the colonel, getting up and frowning at his boots, "I am not sure that I understand."

"Colonel," said Father Brown, "I tell you that this archangel of impudence who stole your forks walked up and down this passage twenty times in the blaze of all the lamps, in the glare of all the eyes. He did not go and hide in dim corners where suspicion might have searched for him. He kept constantly on the move in the lighted corridors, and everywhere that he went he seemed to be there by right. Don't ask me what he was like; you have seen him yourself six or seven times to-night. You were waiting with all the other grand people in the reception room at the end of the passage there, with the terrace just beyond. Whenever he came among you gentlemen, he came in the lightning style of a waiter, with bent head, flapping napkin and flying feet. He shot out on to the terrace, did something to the table cloth, and shot back again towards the office and the waiters' quarters. By the time he had come under the eye of the office clerk and the waiters he had become another man in every inch of his body, in every instinctive gesture. He strolled among the servants with the absent-minded insolence which they have all seen in their patrons. It was no new thing to them that a swell from the dinner party should pace all parts of the house like an animal at the Zoo; they know that nothing marks the Smart Set more than a habit of walking where one chooses. When he was magnificently weary of walking down that particular passage he would wheel round and pace back past the office; in the shadow of the arch just beyond he was altered as by a blast of magic, and went hurrying forward again among the Twelve Fishermen, an ob-sequious attendant. Why should the gentlemen look at a chance waiter? Why should the waiters suspect a first-rate walking gentleman? Once or twice he played the coolest tricks. In the proprietor's pri-vate quarters he called out breezily for a syphon of soda water, saying he was thirsty. He said genially that he would carry it himself, and he did; he carried it quickly and correctly through the thick of you, a waiter with an obvious errand. Of course, it could not have been kept up long, but it only had to be kept up till the end of the fish course.

"His worst moment was when the waiters stood in a row; but even then he con-trived to lean against the wall just round the corner in such a way that for that important instant the waiters thought him a gentleman, while the gentlemen thought him a waiter. The rest went like winking. If any waiter caught him away from the table, that waiter caught a languid aristocrat. He had only to time himself two minutes before the fish was cleared, become a swift servant, and clear it himself. He put the plates down on a sideboard, stuffed the silver in his breast pocket, giving it a bulgy look, and ran like a hare (I heard him coming) till he came to the cloak room. There he had only to be a plutocrat again— a plutocrat called away suddenly on business. He had only to give his ticket to the cloak-room attendant, and go out again elegantly as he had come in. Only—only I happened to be the cloak-room attendant."

"What did you do to him?" cried the colonel, with unusual

intensity. "What did he tell you?"

"I beg your pardon," said the priest immovably, "that is where the story ends."

"And the interesting story begins," muttered Pound. "I think I understand his professional trick. But I don't seem to have got hold of yours."

"I must be going," said Father Brown.

They walked together along the passage to the entrance hall, where they saw the fresh, freckled face of the Duke of Chester, who was bounding buoyantly along towards them.

"Come along, Pound," he cried breathlessly. "I've been looking for you everywhere. The dinner's going again in spanking style, and old Audley has got to make a speech in honour of the forks being saved. We want to start some new ceremony, don't you know, to commemorate the occasion. I say, you really got the goods back, what do you suggest?"

"Why," said the colonel, eyeing him with a certain sardonic approval, "I should suggest that henceforward we wear green coats, instead of black. One never knows what mistakes may arise when one looks so like a waiter."

"Oh, hang it all!" said the young man, "a gentleman never looks like a waiter."

"Nor a waiter like a gentleman, I suppose," said Colonel

Pound, with the same lowering laughter on his face. "Reverend sir, your friend must have been very smart to act the gentleman."

Father Brown buttoned up his commonplace overcoat to the neck, for the night was stormy, and took his commonplace umbrella from the stand.

"Yes," he said; "it must be very hard work to be a gentleman; but, do you know, I have sometimes thought that it may be almost as laborious to be a waiter."

And saying "Good evening," he pushed open the heavy doors of that palace of pleasures. The golden gates closed behind him, and he went at a brisk walk through the damp, dark streets in search of a penny omnibus.

Printed in Great Britain
by Amazon

39143800R00170